The Best
Older Sister

The Best Older Sister

By Sook Nyul Choi

illustrated by
Cornelius Van Wright and Ying-Hwa Hu

A Yearling First Choice Chapter Book

For my daughter Kathleen.

My sincere thanks to Kathy for her inspiration,
to Audrey for her critique,
and to Ingrid van der Leeden
for her enthusiasm and interest in my work.
                              —S.N.C.

To En-wei
and his best older sister,
En-szu .
 —C.V.W. and Y.H.H.

Published by
Bantam Doubleday Dell Publishing Group, Inc.
1540 Broadway
New York, New York 10036
Text copyright © 1997 by Sook Nyul Choi
Illustrations copyright © 1997 by Cornelius Van Wright and Ying-Hwa Hu
All rights reserved.

Library of Congress Cataloging-in-Publication Data
Choi, Sook Nyul.
The best older sister / by Sook Nyul Choi;
illustrated by Cornelius Van Wright and Ying-Hwa Hu.
p.   cm.
"A Yearling first choice chapter book."
Summary: Sunhi is unsettled by the family's focus on her baby brother, but with the
help of her wise grandmother she learns to appreciate her new role of big sister.
ISBN 0-385-32208-9 (hc : alk. paper). —ISBN 0-440-41149-1 (pb : alk. paper)
[1. Brothers and sisters—Fiction. 2. Grandmothers—Fiction.
3. Korean Americans—Fiction.]
I. Van Wright, Cornelius, ill.   II. Hu, Ying-Hwa, ill.   III. Title.
PZ7.C44626   Be 1996
[Fic]–dc20   95-53286   CIP   AC

The trademark Delacorte Press® is registered in the U.S. Patent and Trademark
Office and in other countries.
The trademark Yearling® is registered in the U.S. Patent and Trademark Office
and in other countries.
The text of this book is set in 17-point Baskerville.
Manufactured in the United States of America
February 1997
10 9 8 7 6 5 4 3 2 1

Contents

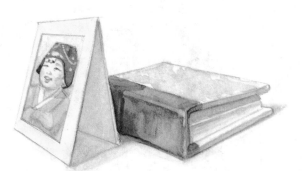

1.
No Time for Sunhi

Sunhi dragged her feet
as she walked home from school.
Her grandmother, Halmoni,
had always waited for Sunhi
outside the schoolyard
with a delicious snack.
Together they would walk home.
Sunhi would tell Halmoni
all about her day at school.

7

But everything changed for Sunhi
when her little brother, Kiju, was born.
Halmoni no longer had time
to play with Sunhi.

Now Halmoni was busy
taking care of Kiju all day
while Sunhi's parents were at work.
Halmoni fed him, bathed him,
and changed his diapers.
That little baby made such a mess
and needed so much attention.

When Sunhi came home,
she saw Halmoni sitting on the sofa,
bouncing Kiju on her knee.
Halmoni was waving Sunhi's
little brown teddy bear
in front of Kiju.

He smiled and drooled with delight.
Mrs. Lee and Mrs. Stone,
their neighbors, were visiting.
They were making silly noises
as they admired the baby.

They hardly noticed Sunhi.

"Oh, hello, Sunhi," said Mrs. Lee,
looking up finally.
"We just stopped by to see Kiju.

How adorable your little brother is!
I can hardly believe he will be
a year old next week."
"Halmoni told us that
it is a Korean custom
to have a big party
on a baby's first birthday,"
said Mrs. Stone.
"You must be so excited."
Sunhi managed a polite smile.
"It is so wonderful to have
a boy in the family," said Mrs. Lee.

Sunhi was tired of all the fuss
everyone made over this baby.

She did not think he was so interesting.
She wished one of these visitors
would adopt him and take him away.

Sunhi glared at the two presents
on the coffee table.
"Sunhi, please put those presents
in your parents' room," said Halmoni.
Sunhi grabbed them and
ran to her parents' room.

She threw them on the bed.
Then she saw three more beautifully
wrapped presents lying in the corner.

"Huh! More presents
for that little boy," said Sunhi.
She could not stand it anymore.

She marched out to the living room
and over to Halmoni.
"Can I have my bear back?
That is still mine, isn't it?"

Sunhi snatched it
and ran back to her room.
Halmoni's eyes opened wide.
She stared after Sunhi.

Sunhi knew she was being rude.
She was ashamed of her behavior
in front of Halmoni and their guests.
But she could not help it.
Tears ran down her cheeks.
She threw herself onto her bed
and sobbed.

Everything was different
with Kiju around.
Even her room
was not her own anymore.
It was full of baby diapers
and baby toys.
It smelled like baby powder.

"How happy you must be to
have a little brother!"
everyone said to Sunhi.
"Isn't it wonderful to be a
big sister now?" they asked.
But it did not seem
so wonderful to Sunhi.
Now her parents had even
less time to talk to her and
play with her in the evenings.
Most of all, Sunhi missed
spending time with Halmoni.
When Halmoni wasn't with Kiju,
she was busy doing things for him.
Just yesterday Sunhi had caught
Halmoni sewing secretly in her room.

Sunhi saw the beautiful blue silk.
She knew that Halmoni must be
making something for Kiju
to wear on his birthday.
"What is so special about this
little baby, anyway?"
Sunhi wondered.
"Why is it so important
to have a boy?
Wasn't I good enough?"
Sunhi sobbed.

2.
A Surprise for Sunhi

There was a gentle knock on the door.
Halmoni entered.
She quietly sat beside Sunhi.
Halmoni wiped Sunhi's tears and
stroked her hair.

Halmoni said,

"I have a surprise for you.

I was going to save it

until next week.

But I think I will give it to you now."

"What is it, Halmoni?" Sunhi said.

She swallowed her tears and

brushed away Halmoni's hand.

"It is in your parents' room.

Three big presents," said Halmoni.

"What? Those are all Kiju's!" said Sunhi.

Halmoni carried the three

big boxes into Sunhi's room.

"Come on, Sunhi. Sit up.

Open this one first," she said.

In the box was a royal blue
silk Korean dress.
It had rainbow-colored sleeves and
butterflies embroidered on the front.
Sunhi loved it.
"This is for you to wear
on Kiju's birthday," said Halmoni.
"I was afraid you saw it last night
when you came to say good night.
These other two are for your
best friends, Jenny and Robin.
Open them and see if you think
they will like them."
Jenny's was peach-colored with
white rosebuds embroidered
on the front.

Robin's was yellow with tiny blue birds
embroidered on the sleeves.
Sunhi knew that her friends
would love these.
"Halmoni, these are so pretty.
It must have taken you a very
long time to make them!"
said Sunhi.

"Well, luckily Kiju is a good baby.

He sleeps a lot.

I am sorry I haven't taken you

to school and picked you up.

I have missed that.

You are special to me.

It is just that babies are

so helpless and need a lot of care.

Just like you when you were

a baby," said Halmoni.

"Did people come and visit and

make such a big fuss over me?"

asked Sunhi.

"Oh, even more!" said Halmoni.

"What a fuss we all made!

Don't you remember the pictures
of your first birthday?
I was in Korea, but your parents
sent me a big batch of pictures
of you every week.
For your birthday, I made you an outfit
and mailed it to your mother."

"I remember those pictures," said Sunhi.

"Now that you are a big sister,"
said Halmoni, "I thought you
could host Kiju's birthday party.

You, Jenny, and Robin can decorate
the birthday table and host together.
Why don't you invite them over?
We can give them their presents,"
said Halmoni.
Sunhi nodded.
"Okay, I'll ask them to come home
with me tomorrow," she said.
"Where is Kiju?"
Halmoni smiled.
"I think he is sleeping.
Let's go see."

3.
A Bad Older Sister

Halmoni and Sunhi walked to
Sunhi's parents' room.
They peered into Kiju's crib.
Kiju was wide awake and playing
happily with his feet.
He was a peaceful, handsome baby.
"Kiju is lucky to have
a big sister like you," said Halmoni.
"Soon he will be walking and talking.
He will follow you all around.
You will have to teach him
to be smart and kind just like you."
Sunhi's face turned red.

"Halmoni, I was stupid and mean.
Sometimes I wanted
to be an only child again.

I have been a bad older sister,"
said Sunhi.

"Sunhi, that is all right," said Halmoni.
"It is hard to get used to
having a baby in the house.
Sometimes we wish
things had not changed.
But that doesn't mean we are bad.
I know that you love Kiju very much.
I know you are going to be
the best older sister."
Sunhi watched Kiju.

She promised herself
that she would give him the best
first birthday party ever.
"What is Kiju's
birthday outfit like?" asked Sunhi.
"It is just a silk outfit much like
the one you wore," said Sunhi's mother,
walking into the room.
"He is not wearing
an extra-special outfit?
He isn't more special
and important because
he is a boy?" asked Sunhi.
"Of course not!
You are both equally special,"
said Sunhi's mother.

She hugged Sunhi.
Halmoni took Sunhi's hand
in her own. She said,
"Is your right eye more special and
important than your left eye?"
Halmoni had lots of funny sayings
like this, but Sunhi understood.

The next day Jenny and Robin
came over. All three girls
tried on their outfits.
"Ooooh, thank you, Halmoni," Jenny said.
Robin said, "Oh, how pretty! Thank you."
Halmoni beamed with joy.

Then they looked at pictures
of Sunhi's first birthday.
They all laughed at the funny faces
Sunhi made in the pictures.
They laughed and laughed and
rolled on the floor.

4.
The Best
First Birthday Party

On the morning of Kiju's birthday
Jenny and Robin came over very early.
Sunhi's father unfolded
the embroidered silk screen.
Sunhi's mother spread out
a beautiful silk tablecloth.
Halmoni brought out rice cakes.
Halmoni started placing
one green rice cake on top of another.
"See, you stack them just like you stack
pebbles at the beach," she said.

Sunhi began stacking the white
rice cakes. She mixed them
with green rice cakes
to make a pretty design.

Robin stacked the bright red apples.
Jenny stacked brown rice cakes
into a tall tower.
Finally the big table was all set.

The girls helped Halmoni dress Kiju.
They put silk trousers, a silk shirt,
and a green silk jacket on him.
A big, pointy black hat
went on his head.

All their friends and relatives
arrived. The girls placed Kiju
in his high chair at the table.
Kiju cooed and reached for
the colorful goodies.

Jenny, Robin, and Sunhi made
funny faces to get Kiju to smile
and look at the camera.
Sunhi's father hurried to take
as many pictures as he could.

"Take lots of pictures of the
beautiful table the girls decorated,"
said Sunhi's mother.
Then, Jenny, Robin, and Sunhi
saw the sign at the front of the table.

"Decorated by Jenny, Robin, and Sunhi,"
it said in Sunhi's mother's printing.
Sunhi smiled at her mother,
and her mother smiled back.
All three girls gazed at the table proudly.

Decorated
by
Jenny
Robin
and
Sunhi

"Don't move.

I want a picture of all of you,"

said Sunhi's father.

"Wait!" Sunhi dragged

Jenny and Robin

behind the table.

Then she picked up Kiju and

gave him a big squeeze.

She held him up to pose

for the camera.

Sunhi's father quickly took

a picture of them.

Then Kiju started to squirm

and struggle to be free.

Sunhi put him down.

He tore off his birthday hat
and scrambled toward his
shiny rattle on the floor.
Everyone laughed.

Sunhi's mother lifted Kiju up high.

Kiju said, "Woooh, woooh."

He looked at everyone with a big smile.

"He is lots of fun," said Robin.

"Is he hard to take care of?"
asked Jenny.

"Oh, no, he is not so bad," Sunhi said.

She looked at Kiju proudly.

Halmoni watched Sunhi and smiled.

About the Author

Sook Nyul Choi was born and raised in Korea. After immigrating to the United States, she graduated from Manhattanville College, then worked as a teacher for almost twenty years while raising her two daughters. She is the author of four previous children's books, including the award-winning novel *Year of Impossible Goodbyes*. Ms. Choi lives in Cambridge, Massachusetts.

About the Illustrators

Cornelius Van Wright and **Ying-Hwa Hu** are a husband-and-wife team who live in New York City with their two children. Mr. Van Wright was born in New York and studied at the School of Art and Design and the School of Visual Arts. Ms. Hu, born in Taipei, Taiwan, studied at Shi Chen College and St. Cloud State University. The couple have illustrated numerous children's books both together and individually.